A Note to Parents

For many children, learning math is difficult and "I hate math!" is their first response—to which many parents silently add "Me, too!" Children often see adults comfortably reading and writing, but they rarely have such models for mathematics. And math fear can be catching!

The easy-to-read stories in this **Hello Math** series were written to give children a positive introduction to mathematics, and parents a pleasurable re-acquaintance with a subject that is important to everyone's life. **Hello Math** stories make mathematical ideas accessible, interesting, and fun for children. The activities and suggestions at the end of each book provide parents with a hands-on approach to help children develop mathematical interest and confidence.

Enjoy the mathematics!

• Give your child a chance to retell the story. The more familiar children are with the story, the more they will understand its mathematical concepts.

• Use the colorful illustrations to help children "hear and see" the math at work in the story.

• Treat the math activities as games to be played for fun. Follow your child's lead. Spend time on those activities that engage your child's interest and curiosity.

• Activities, especially ones using physical materials, help make abstract mathematical ideas concrete.

Learning is a messy process. Learning about math calls for children to become immersed in lively experiences that help them make sense of mathematical concepts and symbols.

Although learning about numbers is basic to math, other ideas, such as identifying shapes and patterns, measuring, collecting and interpreting data, reasoning logically, and thinking about chance, are also important. By reading these stories and having fun with the activities, you will help your child enthusiastically say "**Hello, Math**," instead of "I hate math."

—Marilyn Burns
National Mathematics Educator
Author of *The I Hate Mathematics! Book*

To Joey
— G.M.

For Sophi
— D.N.

Copyright © 1997 by Scholastic Inc.
The activities on pages 28-32 copyright ©1997 Marilyn Burns.
All rights reserved. Published by Scholastic Inc.
CARTWHEEL BOOKS and the CARTWHEEL BOOKS logo
are registered trademarks of Scholastic Inc.
HELLO MATH READER and the HELLO MATH READER logo
are trademarks of Scholastic Inc.

Library of Congress Cataloging-in-Publication Data

Maccarone, Grace.
    Three pigs, one wolf, and seven magic shapes / by Grace Maccarone;
    illustrated by David Neuhaus; math activities by Marilyn Burns.
       p.   cm.— (Hello math reader. Level 3)
    Summary: Tells the story of three pigs who acquire some magic shapes, which they
use for various purposes, some smart and some not so smart. Includes a section with related activities.
    ISBN 0-590-30857-2
    [1. Shape — Fiction. 2. Tangrams — Fiction. 3. Pigs — Fiction.
      4. Characters in literature — Fiction.]
I. Neuhaus, David, ill. II. Burns, Marilyn
    III. Title. IV. Series.
PZ7.M4784115Fo 1997
[E] — dc21
                      97-5040
                      CIP
                      AC

12 11 10 9   0/0 01 02

Printed in the U.S.A.   23

First Scholastic printing, December 1997

Three Pigs, One Wolf, and Seven Magic Shapes

by Grace Maccarone
Illustrated by David Neuhaus
Math Activities by Marilyn Burns

Hello Math Reader — Level 3

Cartwheel
·B·O·O·K·S·®
SCHOLASTIC INC.
New York Toronto London Auckland Sydney

Do you know a story about three little pigs? Of course you do. They built three little houses—out of straw, sticks, and bricks. Then the Big Bad Wolf came along and huffed and puffed and blew two houses down. Only the brick house was strong and safe. So two of the pigs were eaten and the third pig lived happily ever after.

In a nearby village, three other little pigs were ready to seek their fortunes. They kissed their mama and papa good-bye and went their separate ways.

Now, the first little pig met a magic duck.

"Please, duck, can you help me seek my fortune?" said the pig.

And the duck gave the first little pig seven magic shapes—two little triangles, one medium-sized triangle, two large triangles, a square, and a parallelogram.

"Use them wisely," said the duck, and he walked away.

As the pig went along with his seven shapes, he grew lonely. After all, at home he had a brother and a sister pig to talk to and play with. So he used his magic shapes to make a cat.

"This is very wise," said the pig, "for I will not be lonely anymore."

Just then, guess who came by? Big Brad Wolf! He's the twin brother of the wolf in the other three-pig story. Big Brad had run all the way from the other village, so he was doing a lot of huffing and puffing. He huffed and he puffed and he puffed and he huffed. Then he ate up the little pig, and the cat, too!

The second little pig met a magic rabbit.

"Please, rabbit, can you help me seek my fortune?" said the pig.

And the rabbit gave the second little pig seven magic shapes—two little triangles, one medium-sized triangle, two large triangles, a square, and a parallelogram.

"Use them wisely," said the rabbit, and she hopped away.

That evening, as it grew dark, the pig grew frightened. He used his magic shapes to make a candle.

"This is very wise," said the pig, "for I will not be frightened anymore."

But it wasn't wise enough.

Along came the wolf, who huffed and
puffed and puffed and huffed and blew the candle
out. And he ate up the pig.

The third little pig met a magic swan.

"Please, swan, can you help me find my fortune?" asked the pig.

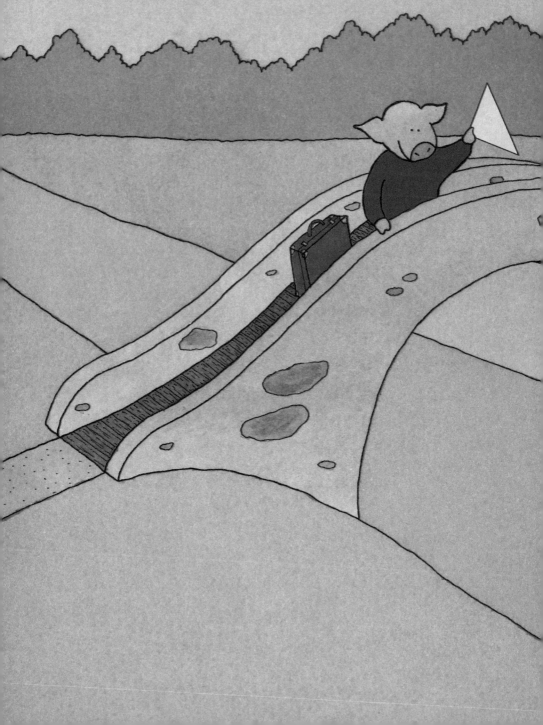

So the swan gave the third little pig seven magic shapes—two little triangles, one medium-sized triangle, two large triangles, a square, and a parallelogram.

"Use them wisely," said the swan, and he swam away.

Now, the third little pig thought and thought and thought about how to use the shapes wisely. She decided to build a safe and cozy house. That was a very smart thing to do because just then the wolf came—and he was still hungry!

He saw the pig's house and said, "Little pig, little pig, let me come in."

"No, no, not by the hair of my chinny chin chin," said the pig.

"Then I'll huff and I'll puff and I'll blow your house in," said the wolf.

Well, he huffed and he puffed and he puffed and he huffed, but he could not blow the house in.

So he went away.

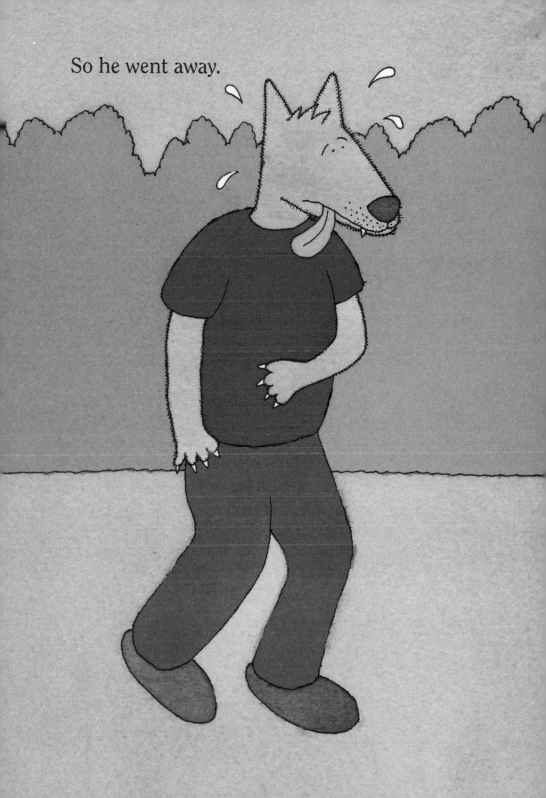

But that's not the end of the story.

One day, the pig who built a house of bricks met the pig who built a house of shapes. They fell in love and were married and they no longer needed two houses.

The pig who built a house of shapes had an idea. She took apart her house and used the seven shapes to build a beautiful sailboat that would take her and her mate on a long honeymoon.

The two pigs had just boarded the boat when Big Brad Wolf suddenly returned—very angry and very hungry. So he huffed and he puffed and he puffed and he huffed. He made a wonderful wind that kept the boat sailing halfway around the world.

And the two little pigs lived happily ever after
and had three little pigs of their own — and all of
them were very smart.

• ABOUT THE ACTIVITIES •

The tangram is an ancient Chinese puzzle that uses seven pieces cut from a square. These pieces include two small triangles, one medium-sized triangle, two large triangles, one square, and one parallelogram.

Once they're cut, putting the seven pieces back together to make the square (without looking at how the square was cut) is surprisingly tricky for some people. It also can be challenging to arrange pieces into other common geometric shapes—a triangle or a rectangle, for example.

But the special charm of the tangram is that its pieces can be arranged into many delightful shapes. And while making shapes engages your child, it also gives them important experience with geometry. By experimenting with tangram pieces, children become familiar with how these particular geometric shapes can be put together and taken apart to make many other shapes. Children not only enjoy these explorations, but receive valuable preparation for learning about polygons, congru- ence, similarity, angles, area, perimeter, and other geometric ideas.

The activities that follow suggest some of the shapes you and your child can make together. Cut out the tangram pieces on the back cover. Experiment along with your child, and have fun doing the math!

—Marilyn Burns

You'll find tips and suggestions
for guiding the activities whenever
you see a box like this!

Cutting Out the Tangram

The tangram pieces on the back cover fit together to make a square. Cut out the pieces. Be careful to cut on the lines. Count to make sure you have seven pieces.

Find all of the triangles. How many do you have?

The two small triangles are the same size. Put one on top of the other to check.

There is one medium-sized triangle. Figure out which one this is. How did you do it?

The two big triangles left are the same size. Put one on top of the other to check.

You should have one square. The last piece has a hard name to read. It is called a parallelogram. Ask an adult for help saying it.

Count to be sure you have all seven pieces.

Set the pieces aside but keep them nearby. You'll need them as you look through the book again.

Retelling the Story

How is this story different from the story you know about the three little pigs?

Opposite the page where the first little pig met a magic duck, there is a square put together with the tangram pieces. See if you can fit your seven pieces together to make a square.

> This may be too difficult for your child. If so, then trace the appropriate pieces on a sheet of blank paper so that your child can match the actual pieces as with tho square. Use other sheets of paper to trace around the other shapes to make puzzles that match the shapes in the book.

Can you use your seven pieces to make the magic duck? You can't place them on the picture in the book because that duck is too small for your pieces. Here's a hint to get you started: The duck's head is the medium-sized triangle.

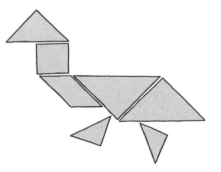

The first little pig used the magic pieces to make a cat to play with. Can you make the cat with your seven pieces?

What did the wolf do to the cat and the pig?

The second little pig met a magic rabbit. Can you make the rabbit with your seven pieces?

What shapes are the rabbit's ears?

Why did the second little pig use the magic pieces to make a candle? Can you make the candle with your pieces?

What shape is at the bottom?

What shape is the flame?

What did the wolf do to the candle and the pig?

The third little pig met a magic swan. Can you make the swan with your seven pieces?

The third little pig built a house with the magic pieces. Can you make the house with your seven pieces?

What shape is the chimney of the house?

What happened when the wolf tried to blow in the house?

Then the third little pig made a sailboat. Can you make the sail-boat with your seven pieces?

What shapes did you use for the big sail?

What shapes did you use for the small sail?

What shapes did you use for the rest of the boat?

Other Tangram Shapes

There are many, many shapes you can make. Here are some to try.

Make one of these shapes on a piece of paper using your seven pieces. Then trace around it to make another puzzle. Either trace around each piece or around the whole shape. Take your pieces off. Now try to put them back on.

Do the same for the other shapes.

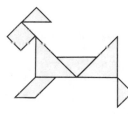

dog

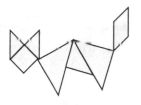

cat

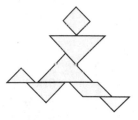

running man

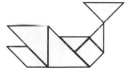

whale

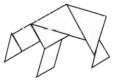

bear

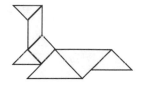

seal

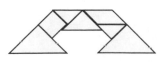

bridge

seven

T

Make a Tangram Puzzle

Use your seven pieces to make a shape that you like on a piece of blank paper. Be sure to place pieces so there is no overlapping. Think of a name for your shape and write it on the paper.

Have someone trace around each piece or have someone hold each piece in place as you trace around it.

Take off your pieces. Now try to put them back on your puzzle.

Make other puzzles.

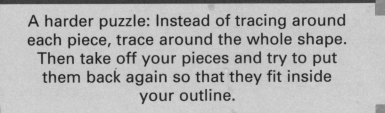

A harder puzzle: Instead of tracing around each piece, trace around the whole shape. Then take off your pieces and try to put them back again so that they fit inside your outline.

Which Piece Is Missing?

This is a game for two people.

One of you builds a shape using all seven pieces. Remember, no overlapping.

Then the other player covers his or her eyes or turns around so that he or she can't see the shape.

The first player takes away one piece without moving the other six pieces.

The other player then looks and says the name of the missing piece.

Take turns.